The Ice Horse

The Ice Horse

Candace Christiansen / paintings by Thomas Locker

Dial Books New York

To John Christiansen

C.C. and T.L.

Published by Dial Books
A Division of Penguin Books USA Inc.
375 Hudson Street
New York, New York 10014

Text copyright © 1993 by Candace Christiansen
Pictures copyright © 1993 by Thomas Locker
All rights reserved
Design by Nancy R. Leo
Printed in the U.S.A.
First Edition
1 3 5 7 9 10 8 6 4 2

Library of Congress Cataloging in Publication Data
Christiansen, Candace.
The ice horse / by Candace Christiansen ; pictures by Thomas Locker.
p.   cm.
Summary: While harvesting ice on the Hudson River with his uncle one winter,
a boy uses quick thinking to save his uncle's horse.
ISBN 0-8037-1400-9.—ISBN 0-8037-1401-7 (lib. bdg.)
[1. Ice industry—Fiction. 2. Horses—Fiction.]   I. Locker, Thomas, 1937–   ill. II. Title.
PZ7.C45287Ic 1993   [E]—dc20   92-28964   CIP   AC

*The art for each picture consists of an oil painting that is
color-separated and reproduced in full color.*

My family and I live on the banks of the Hudson River in a place thickly overgrown with wild roses, irises, and bittersweet vines. We often walk along the river and sometimes we explore the coves and inlets from a small boat. Once we went ashore and discovered the ruins of an old building. As we walked around it, we were astonished at how large the foundation was, and so we tried to find out what the building could have been used for.

We discovered that the ruins are what is left of the Newtonhook Icehouse. One old man we met there told us that back before there were refrigerators people harvested ice wherever the winters were cold enough to freeze rivers and lakes. He said that all the ice for the city of New York came from the Newtonhook Icehouse and other icehouses like it along the river. He remembered the ice harvests on the river very well for he had taken part in them when he was a boy. This story is about the first winter he helped harvest the ice. . . .

C. C.

A heavy frost set in by late November, the winter I turned twelve. Soon everyone who lived by the river would be getting ready for the ice harvest. Men would come from miles around with teams of horses, plows, and ice saws, waiting for the river to freeze. Already wagons from a nearby sawmill rumbled into town laden with sawdust. The men shoveled it into large piles near the icehouse. Later it would be used to keep the blocks of ice from melting and sticking together. My uncle Joe, who delivered ice to people in the city, would be coming to stay with my family and help us harvest the ice.

After school one day I heard the blast of the steamboat whistle, and I raced over to the dock. It was crowded with horses, stamping and whinnying as they came ashore. Right away I saw Uncle Joe with his horse Max. He waved to me and I ran over to meet him. "Why don't you take Max up to the barn, Jack," he said, giving me a hug. He'd never asked me to help before, and so feeling very proud, I got in line with the men who were leading their horses to the stable.

When we got to the barn, I helped brush and feed Max. I loved the smell of his warm coat. As we worked, Uncle Joe said that if the cold weather held, the river would soon be ready. When the ice was about two feet thick, it would be safe and you could drive a team clear across from one side to the other.

"Let's hope the river is good to everyone this year," he added. I wasn't sure what he meant then, although I came to understand it well before that winter ended.

For the next few days after school I helped Uncle Joe sharpen his ice saws. He said when the harvest began I could plow the snow that covered the ice too. I could hardly wait.

By the end of the week winter had really set in. The river turned to stone, and mountain farmers came across the frozen river with their teams of horses to work at the icehouse.

The horses were fitted with spiked horse-shoes so they wouldn't slip on the ice. As he hitched up Max, Uncle Joe hung a thick rope around the horse's neck, bringing the end of it back along beside the reins. "If Max ever falls through the ice, hang on to this rope and pull hard," my uncle said. "It will choke him, but it may save his life."

"How can choking him save him?" I asked, horrified. Uncle Joe patted Max's neck and said soberly, "It's the only way to stop him from thrashing around so we can help him. He can't climb out of the water by himself."

It wasn't long after that, that a shout came up from the river: "The ice is ready!" The wind howled down the valley as the men began to plow. Behind them the snow swirled into glistening drifts. After the ice was cleared, Uncle Joe and I attached a special tool to the harness that would be used to mark the ice into blocks. Then, with Max leading the way, we stepped out onto the frozen river in the blinding winter sun.

By the end of the week a channel had been cut through the center of the river. Day after day Uncle Joe and I stood out on the ice with the others, sawing the ice into blocks. Men pushed the blocks of ice with poles, through the channel and down to conveyor belts that carried the blocks up into the icehouses.

One night while we were feeding Max, Uncle Joe said, "It's my turn to keep the channel open tonight. Your dad said that you could come along too." After dinner we climbed into the boat, and Uncle Joe slowly rowed us back and forth to keep the water from freezing over. He talked about the hot summer days when he and Max delivered ice in the city. I rocked the boat from side to side, making waves so the ice wouldn't form.

The ice harvest continued for weeks and as spring approached, the days began to grow longer. The men worked harder and faster each day to harvest as much ice as possible before the ice became too thin. Now Uncle Joe spent more time inside the icehouse, stacking ice blocks and covering them with sawdust. Often I had to plow the snow that had fallen over-night by myself. Max and I had become a team.

One cloudy afternoon when I was plowing, I got too close to the channel's edge. Suddenly the ice shattered beneath Max with a loud crack. It gave way and Max reared, tipping the plow over and throwing me to one side. Max snorted as he struggled to get up on the ice, but he fell back down, disappearing into the black, cold water!

I shouted frantically and several men ran over to help, but the ice wasn't strong enough to hold them. Then I saw the end of the thick rope that went around Max's neck. Remembering what Uncle Joe had told me, I crawled out onto the thin ice. I grabbed the rope and pulled on it for all I was worth. In a few moments I felt Max go limp. I hung on to the rope, tugging for dear life. Finally Uncle Joe and some of the men arrived with long planks and ropes. They began to haul Max out.

At first Max just lay there and I thought I'd choked him to death or that he had drowned. But then he stood up and began shaking himself. I was still scared and trembling, but Uncle Joe put his arm around me and said, "Don't feel bad, Jack. It can happen to anyone. Max will be fine—he's taken a dip before."

It wasn't long before the river flooded and the ice harvest ended. Each day now, some of the ice cutters were packing up and leaving town. Finally, just as my spring vacation was about to begin, my father said, "You better go down to the dock, Jack. Uncle Joe is packing up to leave." I walked slowly down the road and as I rounded the bend, there he was—and behind him was my own red trunk!

"I could use some help delivering ice in the city for a couple of weeks," he said. His eyes sparkled and he patted my shoulder. "How about it?"

So I worked with Uncle Joe in the city that spring, and then later during the summer. And I knew I'd be ready to work in the ice harvest when the river froze again the next winter.